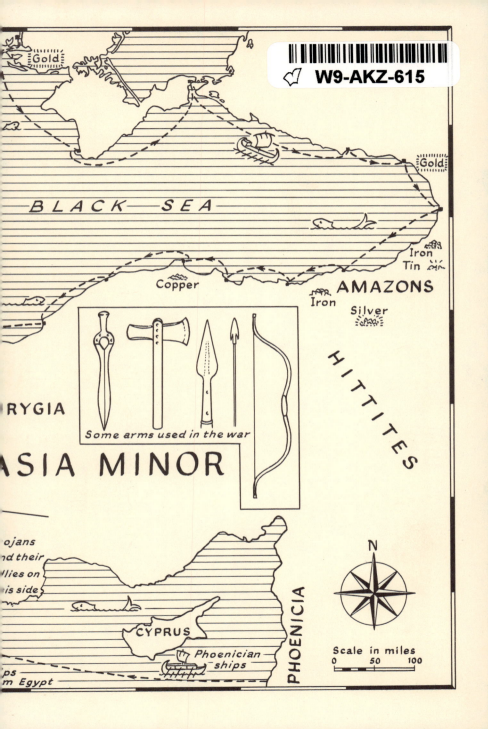

Gold

BLACK SEA

Gold

Iron
Tin

Copper

Iron AMAZONS

Silver

HITTITES

RYGIA

Some arms used in the war

ASIA MINOR

ojans
nd their
lies on
is side

CYPRUS

Phoenician
ships

PHOENICIA

N

Scale in miles
0   50   100

ps
m Egypt

For Laura with love Xmas '74
Aunt Katie

The Windswept City

BOOKS BY HENRY TREECE

SPLINTERED SWORD
THE CENTURION
THE WINDSWEPT CITY

MEREDITH PRESS NEW YORK

The Windswept City

A Novel of the Trojan War

By Henry Treece

Illustrations by Faith Jaques

Library of Congress Catalog Card Number: 67-20860 Manufactured in the United States of America for Meredith Press

About This Book 🐚

The story of the Trojan War was first told by the blind poet Homer almost three thousand years ago. His great book is called the *Iliad,* and in it he describes how the Greeks sailed to Troy and besieged that windswept city for ten years. They did this for revenge, because a Trojan prince named Paris had enticed a Greek queen named Helen away from her family in Sparta. At the end of the war Troy was burned down, the Trojan leaders were mostly killed, and Helen was forgiven by her husband and taken back to Sparta.

Ancient historians said that all this happened about 1180 B.C. But although Homer described where Troy was—that is, near the sea, close to the Hellespont straits, at the edge of the Trojan plain, beside the winding river Scamander, with Mount Ida towering up behind it—later people thought that it was all a fairy tale.

But less than a hundred years ago, in 1871, a German merchant-scholar named Schliemann decided to see if he could find Troy. He went to the place Homer had described, which is now in Turkey, and three miles from the sea found a man-made mound over 160 feet high. Its name was Hissarlik, but he felt sure that it was Troy—and he was right.

As his workmen dug down they found many ancient walls of limestone and streets, just as Homer had said. They found ten cities in all, one built on the other through the centuries. The second one from the bottom was covered with ashes, as though it had been burned down once upon a time, and Schliemann was quite certain that he had discovered the city where the war had taken place. And in this city he also found golden treasure that he felt was from the fortress where Helen once had lived.

But—and this is the *interesting* point—though

all the experts had laughed at Schliemann the mer-
chant when he started, once he had found Troy they
began to consider the *whole* Trojan War with great
seriousness, and they came up with some exciting
facts:

(1) that this war *had* happened, because the Trojans had stopped the Greeks from sailing up the
Hellespont to trade for gold in the Black Sea
area;

(2) that the Greeks, who hated the prosperous Trojans, had camped at the mouth of the river Scamander to stop any Mediterranean merchants
from bringing trade to Troy.

If you look at the map on pages 42 and 43, you
will see what this means.

Two more things: These later historians rather
ruin the romantic side of the story! They say that
the war didn't last for ten years but that the Greeks
had been raiding the coast of Asia Minor for that
length of time, and that the siege of Troy was only
ten *months* long. But, worse than that, they think
that the Greeks were more interested in their trade
than in Helen. She was only the excuse for them to
destroy Troy!

Finally, it was first said that the Greeks got into
Troy inside the hollow model of a horse. But many

historians—even of old times—thought that this did not make sense. It would have to be a very big "horse" to get even a small army inside it.

You will have to read this story to see what probably happened!

H. T.

Contents

GREEKS AND TROJANS

GREEKS

(They prayed to Zeus, Hera, Athene, and Hermes.)

AGAMEMNON:	*King of Mycenae, High King of Achaea, the Greek leader*
MENELAUS:	*King of Sparta, Agamemnon's brother, husband of Helen*
ACHILLES:	*Prince of Thessaly, leader of Myrmidon army*
ODYSSEUS:	*King of Ithaca, the most cunning of the Greeks*
PATROCLUS:	*The dearest friend of Achilles, killed by Hector of Troy*

AJAX: *King of Salamis*
PALAMEDES: *Greek hero, betrayed and murdered by Odysseus*

(Other important Greeks are Idomeneus, King of Crete; Machaon, surgeon to the Greek forces; Nestor, King of Pylus, the oldest leader in the war; Teucer, the half brother of Ajax, a famous archer; Diomedes, King of Argos and second-in-command of the Greeks. But these men do not come into this story.)

TROJANS

(They prayed to Zeus, Apollo, Aphrodite, and Artemis.)

PRIAM: *King of Troy, an old man*
HECABE: *Queen of Troy (called Hecuba by the Romans)*
HECTOR: *Eldest son of Priam and leader of the Trojans in war*
PARIS: *Younger son of Priam; he stole Helen from Sparta and was brother to Hector*
CASSANDRA: *Daughter of Priam, sister of Hector and Paris; she was a prophetess whom no one believed*
AENEAS: *Cousin of Hector and Paris, second-in-command of the Trojan army; son of old Anchises*
HELEN OF TROY: *Wife of King Menelaus, Queen of Sparta, though she lived for ten years in the city of Troy*

The Windswept City

1 Greek Treachery

Asterius, the slave boy, crouched under the thick laurel bush and shivered. The sea lay before him and the gurgling river Scamander to his left. It was a very cold night with a bright round white moon above him, staring down, watching him. The goddess Artemis was in that moon with her bow and arrows, perhaps being cross with him for coming down from Troy to watch the Greeks. An owl fluttered by the laurel on slow wings, almost flapping into his face. He drew back and shut his eyes. He felt sure that the owl was Hera, the oldest goddess, come to spy on him and give him away to the terrible Greeks.

He said a prayer: "O Hera, forgive me. I am not really a Trojan spy. My name is Asterius and I only live in Troy because my mistress, the lady Helen, lives there too. I was born in Thrace, not Troy, goddess. I only came down to see what Greeks were like. Forgive me."

The owl gave a loud squawk and fluttered away. Asterius opened his dark eyes and wrapped his blue cloak around him because the chilly wind from the sea was blowing up again. He did not really expect that the owl would forgive him, if it was Hera, because she was the goddess who looked after Greeks. So he shut his eyes again and said another prayer: "O Aphrodite, O Apollo, O Artemis, protect me,

please. I think that the old witch Hera is after me.
If you let me get back safely up the secret water pipe,
tomorrow I will leave my best bronze knife at the
shrine for you. I swear it."

When he had said this and opened his eyes again,
he began to shake worse than ever, because just two
paces away in the moonlight, with his back toward
the bush, stood a man. At first Asterius thought it
must be the king of all gods, Zeus himself, come to
fetch him for not offering the bronze knife to
him. Then in the moonlight he saw that the man wore
a leather helmet with boar's tusks sticking up from
either side, and a ragged leather tunic that rustled
when he moved his thick body. There was a broad-
bladed bronze sword hanging down at the back of his
belt, swinging from side to side. When the man turned,
Asterius saw that he carried a long shield covered with
oxhide on his left arm. So this wasn't Zeus. Zeus
would have been clothed in gold, and he would be
much taller and handsomer than this squat man with
rough black beard all over his cheeks and throat.

Suddenly the man turned and seemed to look right
into the bush where he lay crouched. His eyes were
wide and staring and the shadows thrown down by
the moon made him look like a fierce animal. For a
moment Asterius thought the man was going to pull
the sword out of his belt and poke into the bush, but

then he turned away and went slowly down the stony slope toward the Greek camp.

Asterius watched him and saw the cluster of wind-blown hide tents that flapped in the sea breeze; and beyond that he saw the tall oak stockade, behind which the Greek ships were drawn up. It was like a city in itself, all the black-painted ships lying side by side, like houses along streets. Here and there stood mounds of earth where the Greeks had buried their chiefs after the fighting along the shore. Sea-birds were swooping over the mounds, crying out, and Asterius thought that these were the chiefs come back to keep an eye on things.

He thought he would creep through the bush as soon as he could and run all the three miles back to Troy. But suddenly the man in the boar helmet turned back toward him and whistled with his thick fingers in his mouth, and out of the shadows by the nearest mound two slaves came running, carrying a heavy clinking sack.

The man in the helmet said hoarsely, "Quick, you fools, or Palamedes will be back from hunting. If he catches you at it, don't expect me to stand up for you. Throw the bag of gold into his tent and be off with you now."

One of the slaves said humbly, "Yes, great Odys-

seus, we will be quick. Do not forget the reward you
promised us, King of Ithaca."

Asterius clenched his fists tight, drawing himself in
as small as he could with fear, to think that the savage sea-rover Odysseus had stood so close to him. This
was the craftiest man in the world, the Trojans said,
and one of the fiercest. Few dared stand against him
in battle—and he had been only two paces away
from the bush.

Asterius wondered whether he ought to offer his
necklace of blue beads to Zeus, on condition that the
god got him safely back into the city. They were
such pretty beads and had come from Egypt in the
ship of an old Phoenician who often brought beautiful things for the lady Helen. When she gave the
beads to Asterius she said, "Now that you are eleven,
you are old enough to wear something valuable. I
have owned you nearly a year, so you deserve a pres-

ent. Take care of these beads; they cost me three
sheep. When you wear them, the Trojans will know
them."

He was still thinking about this when a horn
sounded beyond the stockade, and three men came
riding up on shaggy ponies, their leather cloaks flapping, long boar spears in their hands. The leader was
a tall young man with fair hair and a faded pointed
blue cap on his head. Behind the riders ran six slaves,
holding in great hounds on leashes. One of the riders
called out to the leader, "Hey, Palamedes, have you
no wine to offer us after our long ride?"

The man in the blue cap laughed and said, "Come
into my tent, friends, and you shall quench your
thirst. I got a shipload of wine from Crete only
three days ago. The word must have gone around,
you cunning rogues!"

The three Greeks went laughing into the hide tent,

and after a short while Asterius saw a torch flare up
inside, and then heard the men laughing again. They
sounded so merry he wished he could be with them
to hear what they were saying.

Then all at once, from behind the other tents,
Odysseus came striding and waving his arms. Following him came a score of lords and warriors, carrying shields and long spears. Odysseus was shouting
at the top of his voice, "I tell you, Palamedes is a traitor. He has received gold from the Trojans. He has
promised to betray us to them. Go, search his tent if
you do not believe me. When have I ever lied to you,
Agamemnon? Did you ever know me to lie, Menelaus?"

Asterius could not see Agamemnon and Menelaus.
He had often heard people talking about them in
Troy, whispering their names as though they were
too fearsome to speak aloud—and now he could not
see them. He could not go back to Troy and tell the
other boy slaves he had seen the King of Mycenae
and his brother, the King of Sparta. He almost wept
with disappointment.

Then something happened that drove these
thoughts away. Palamedes was standing in the doorway of the hide tent, a wine cup in his right hand. He
was laughing and saying, "Come in, my lords, and
share the wine. This is a surprise visit. I thought you

were down the coast, foraging among the shore villages. And you, old Odysseus, what brings you out on
such a raw night? I thought you would be in your
tent, playing dice with your thin-lipped friend, Achilles. Have you still got the ivory dice I made for you,
Crafty One?"

Odysseus gave a roar like a lion and suddenly
clasped the arms of Palamedes to his side. "Search
his tent, Agamemnon," he bawled. "Search the traitor's tent."

Four of the soldiers pushed through the flap, bend-
ing low because of the high crests on their bronze helmets, and went inside. Palamedes was still laughing
and joking when they came out again, carrying a
heavy bag. When he saw the bag, Palamedes stopped
laughing and said, "Is this some trick, Agamemnon?
That is not my bag. I have never seen it before."

Asterius heard a deep voice say, "No, it is not your
bag, Palamedes. The stitching around its edge is Trojan work. And the gold inside it is Trojan gold. Odysseus is right, you are a traitor."

Then there was a lot of scuffling and shouting, and
a cloud passed over the moon for a moment. When
the light shone clear again, Asterius saw that Palamedes was lying on the dusty ground outside his tent,
and the soldiers were striking down with their spears
and throwing heavy stones at him.

Asterius wanted to jump up and run to them and tell them that Odysseus had put the gold in the tent; but suddenly he knew that he was too frightened to go toward those fierce soldiers, who seemed more like wild beasts than men. He covered his eyes with his hands and tried to keep quiet. And when all was

very still again, he looked out of the bush and saw that the men had gone away. Palamedes still lay there, with heaps of stones about him. He did not move. Only his leather cloak flapped in the sea wind.

Asterius backed through the bush, and when he was in its shadow, turned and ran like a rabbit toward the hill on which stood the city of Troy. He half expected arrows to come whistling after him, but nothing happened. He was breathless with fear and running when he reached the base of the hill and clambered over the great stones that led up to the lower wall. He had to sit down for a while to get his breath back before he dared push through the bushes and find the secret water pipe that he would have to crawl through to get into the city.

The great Scaean Gates were always barred at nightfall, and even if they weren't, Asterius would not have dared knock on them and face the guard. King Priam had recently brought in some Ethiopians from farther away than Egypt even, and Asterius was afraid of their solemn black faces that looked like carved ebony. He would not dare to face them in daytime, much less at night, though they were supposed to be on Troy's side.

So he wormed his way through the wild lavender and the scrubby gorse, and at last he found the pipe. Not much water flowed down it, but it was very cold inside the stone runnel. He scraped his knuckles and knees climbing up to street level.

No one was about in the mazelike streets, so he jumped down and ran as fast as he could to the palace of Priam. He felt that his mistress, Helen, ought to be told about the murder of Palamedes. He felt he had to tell somebody, because it was so terrible to see a man murdered, even a Greek.

2 Cassandra's Warning

The palace was very dark and still. No guards stood on the great steps that led up through the porch into the vestibule. They would be wrapped in their cloaks, sitting by a brazier at the side of the great hall, he thought. It was such a chilly night.

In the vestibule three women in black robes were chanting and throwing herbs onto a little fire. They had white ash on their heads and were mourning for someone. Asterius thought it must be one of the Trojan lords who had been ambushed a few days before.

Someone was always being ambushed, and Troy was
full of priestesses who wore ash on their heads and
wailed around fires at night. Asterius did not like to
look at them, or to have them look at him. Often they
daubed white clay over their faces, and painted
streaks of blue or black across their cheeks when they
were making offerings, and this sent a shiver down his
back.

So he ran past them as quietly as he could and
along the corridor. Halfway down, a tall guard with
a spear stepped out from behind some hangings and
pushed Asterius against the cold stone wall. "Where
are you going?" he said fiercely.

Asterius said, "Let me through, Atabyrius, I must
speak to my mistress."

The guard tugged at the boy's ear and said, "How do I know you are not a Greek spy with a dagger hidden under your tunic?"

Asterius pulled away from him. "Don't be a fool, Atabyrius," he said. "You know very well who I am."

The guard pretended to be very serious and shook his head. He said, "I know someone who looks a bit like you, a young fellow named Asterius. But an old soldier like me knows better than to let every young fellow go running through the palace because he looks like Asterius. I think you are a spy, disguised to look like Asterius. That's what I think."

Asterius said, "Well, you can soon find out the truth, because my mistress, the lady Helen, is standing right behind you and she will say who I am."

Atabyrius swung around and bowed his head—but, of course, there was no one behind him. And when he realized this, it was too late, because Asterius had dodged around him and was racing along the passageway.

The guard watched him go, then turned back to his post and began to whistle softly to himself to pass the time away.

Asterius ran around two bends in the corridor and then had to pass across an upper courtyard in the middle of which stood an enormous bronze bull with eagle's wings. He had always been afraid of it. The

dark metal gleamed a reddish color in the glow of the
tripod fires that stood about it. The bull's eyes
seemed to glare as though it were alive. Asterius was
edging away from the creature when a woman sud-

denly came from behind the pedestal and stood in
his way. She was wearing a rumpled woolen gown and
her face was thin and pale. Over her uncombed dark
hair she wore a black cloth.

Asterius bowed his head before her because she
was one of the royal house. He said, "Greetings, my
lady Cassandra, daughter of King Priam. I hope you
are well."

The princess gazed at him out of her wide dark eyes and said, "No one is well in Troy, slave. In this doomed city no one will ever be well again. Apollo has spoken to me in my dreams and has told me the end of all things. And it will be a terrible end."

Asterius hated to meet Cassandra in the dark passageway because she always said things like this. He did not know how to speak to her, but he smiled and said, "It is wintertime, my lady, and we are all sad until the spring comes, shut up here in the palace. We shall feel better when the sun is warm again and we can go out."

Cassandra took hold of a lock of his black hair and twisted it in her long white fingers. Then she said, "Troy is doomed. We shall never see the sun again, boy. We shall all die up here on this hill before the summer comes again."

This made Asterius angry. In the stables there was a lovely horse called Hippomedon that belonged to Helen, and the boy planned to ride over the plains on this horse as soon as the weather got better. He said, "Very well, lady, if you are so certain that Troy is doomed, why do you not tell your father, King Priam? Why do you not tell your mother, Queen Hecabe, or your great warrior brothers, Hector and Paris? You could even tell your warrior cousin, Aeneas. Then they could do something about it."

Suddenly Cassandra took him by the hand and
drew him toward the pedestal above which the bronze
bull towered. "Sit with me a little while," she said.
"Do not be afraid; I am not mad, in spite of what
the slave women say about me."

Asterius felt himself blushing because he had heard
the slave women saying this many times. But he did
not dare to answer. Then Cassandra said, quite softly
and in such an ordinary voice that she might have
been talking about a new dress she was having woven
at the looms, or a new pair of sandals made at the
palace workshops, "Asterius, Apollo put a curse on
me long ago and it is this: I am fated to see the
truth of things and to foretell the future, but no one
will ever believe me. Is that not a heavy burden to
carry through life?"

Asterius scratched his neck and said, "Hector
would believe you. Hector is the greatest warrior the
world has ever known. There is no man who could
stand against him, he is so big and strong, so skilled
with his weapons. A hero like that would listen to
you and would save Troy."

All at once he felt something wet on his arm. He
looked up and saw that Cassandra was leaning over
and weeping. He said, "My lady, have I made you
cry? I am sorry. Was it because I spoke of Hector?

Why should you cry because you have a hero as a brother, lady?"

Suddenly Cassandra looked up at him and he backed away from her. He had never seen her eyes look so wide and staring, or her mouth so twisted. He felt quite sure that she was about to put a spell on him, so he bowed hurriedly then turned and almost fled to the high gallery that looked down over the

great hall. He had hoped to find Helen there, perhaps walking alone and singing, but when he looked
into the vast echoing space, he saw that the royal
kindred were gathered in the hall, as though for some
solemn occasion. He did not dare break the silence,
but gazed at them in awe.

King Priam sat in a high-backed chair of Libyan
ebony, his long bronze sword across his knees. He
was an old man now, and his hair and beard were
thin and white. His shoulders were stooped under his
heavy purple cloak, and his hands seemed to shake
like aspen leaves all the time. But his dark eyes were
still bright and his hooked nose curved like the beak
of an eagle. And when he spoke, his voice was as firm
as ever.

Beside his chair, one to left and one to right, stood
his great sons, Hector and Paris. Hector seemed im-
mense in his bronze corselet molded with the shapes
of leaping stags. His arms, in their gold bracelets,
looked like the branches of oak trees, all covered with
curly golden hairs. In the torchlight from the sconces
set along the wall, Asterius saw Hector's light gray
eyes that never missed anything, his straight and
narrow nose, his close-cropped curly hair that looked
like fine bronze itself. He thought that, but for the
sword scars across his face, Hector would be as hand-

some as a god, as handsome as Apollo himself, perhaps.

But not Paris. He was smaller and much darker,
and very restless in all his movements—not steady
and firm as a warrior should be. Paris was more like
a slinger or an archer, not like the highest class of
warrior who used the sword and the javelin. Asterius
wondered why all the women seemed to like Paris
better than Hector. He wondered why Helen, his own
mistress, had ever left her kingdom of Sparta to come
with Paris to live in windswept Troy.

Then, in the gloom, he picked out Helen. She sat
on a lower step, beneath the throne chair, next to
Queen Hecabe, whose gray hair was covered with a
brown shawl and whose old fingers turned continu-
ously at a bone spindle from which the gray wool hung
down. Helen did not seem to be very interested in
what was going on. She seemed to be smiling at some
thought or other in her own head. Asterius wondered
why all the poets said she was so beautiful. Of course
he liked her, because she was as kind to him as a
mother, or an older sister; but that did not make her
beautiful. Long ago, when she had first left her husband Menelaus and her baby daughter Hermione
to sail to Troy with Paris, she might have been
beautiful, for all Asterius knew; but that was ten

years ago. Why, he thought, she must be very old now—she must be nearly thirty.

In the dim torchlight of the hall he thought that her famous golden hair looked faded and dry, and her face thin and sharp. He could see the lines on it when the light caught her from a certain direction. And she frowned too much, which made lines on her brow, and drew her lips downward, which made her look spiteful and shrewish.

Of course her dress was splendid, with all its embroidery in gold and silver threads, and the great diadem she wore, with masses of gold beads hanging down on either side of it, would have bought a whole fleet of ships, or a thousand horses. But that didn't make her beautiful, he thought. Not as beautiful as the poets said.

Then he suddenly felt very mean for thinking these things, because she was the kindest person he had ever known since his parents had died and he was sold into slavery.

He was about to creep away and to dare passing through the Bull Court again when King Priam suddenly spoke up in a loud and angry voice.

3 Trojan Brothers

The King said, "For ten years we have suffered the raids of these Greeks. Now they sit outside our walls like wolves around a farmyard, waiting for the sheep to come forth. Our lives are governed by them. I have grown old, waiting for them to go away."

Hector smiled grimly. "Father," he said, "you knew that this was bound to happen when you closed the Hellespont to them and stopped their ships from sailing to the distant goldfields. And my brother Paris knew it well enough when he stole the lady Helen from Sparta and brought her to live with us here. We all knew that the Greeks were bound to come for

their revenge. We would have done the same our-
selves."

Paris glanced at his brother sharply, then said, "Do
not lay the blame on me. For generations these Greeks
had been putting in to shore and carrying off our own
women. I only did what they had been doing all
along. Besides, my lady Helen wished to come
here. She was tired to death of rocky Sparta, tired
to death of Menelaus, her miserable husband. Is that
not true, Helen?"

Helen did not even glance at him. She said in a
dull voice, "If you say so, Paris. What is there for me
to say now, I who am hardly anything more than a
prisoner in this windy hill-fortress?"

King Priam leaned forward and touched her on
the shoulder. "In the spring," he said, "these Greeks
may sail away for a while, as they usually do, and
then we can move outside the walls and hunt on the
plain down beside the river Scamander. You will feel
better then."

He turned to Hector and said, "I agree with Helen,
we are all prisoners here in Troy. We cannot live the
good life that the gods intended for us, penned up
here like bullocks awaiting the slaughter. You are in
command of the Trojan armies, Hector. Cannot you
and the General Aeneas, your cousin, find some way
of getting rid of these Greeks?"

Hector gazed down calmly at the king. "Father,"
he said in a low voice, "we are in the hands of the
gods, and as you know these Greeks have Pallas
Athene on their side, the goddess of war herself."

Suddenly Helen gave a little laugh and said, "We
pray to Aphrodite, the goddess of love. Surely she can
deal with grim-faced Athene in her silly helmet!"

Paris nodded and said, "My brother makes too
much of a mystery about this war of his. I am not al-
lowed command of the armies, being a younger son,
but I can see three ways of getting rid of the Greeks
forever. First, we should gather all the other peoples
of the land—the Dardanians, Thracians, Mysians,
Phrygians, Carians—to join with us; then, with such
a force, we should make regular attacks and see that
each time we do away with one of their greatest leaders. And when we have shaken their nerve so, we
should make our greatest effort, push past their stockade, and set fire to their black ships as they lie
beached along our shore. That is how it should be
done."

Hector drew in his breath and waited a while before answering. Then he said evenly, "The folk you
mention, these Dardanians and so on, are terrorized
already. The Greeks have burned their villages and
driven away their cattle. They could not come to our

aid even if they wished to, now. If we want allies, then we must send out for real fighting men, for the Hittites from the east."

Priam nodded and said, "I too had thought of that, my son. We will send to them as soon as we can get messengers through the lines. What else have you to say?"

Hector said, smiling now, "As for killing their leaders, I am prepared to play my part in that."

Paris said slyly, "We all know that you have challenged great Achilles—but that he refused to meet you. We know that you have met Ajax in single combat—and that all you two did was to exchange gifts. He gave you the purple shoulder-belt you are wearing now, and you gave him a silver-studded sword. If you ask me, he got the better of the bargain, as Greeks always do. No, I did not mean that sort of thing at all. I meant *real* fighting, dear brother."

Hector's face suddenly became hard. He said starkly, "When you met Menelaus, I do not remember that the poets made songs about it. All I can recall is that you both got tired, leaned on your swords, then turned and went back to your tents. But do not taunt me, brother. I will see that Achilles comes out to meet me. I can assure you of that. And when I have put an end to him, I will challenge Agamemnon himself. Then, perhaps, we can go on with the last stage of your plan and burn the Greek ships as they lie along the shore. So, are you satisfied?"

Paris stood up and arranged his cloak. He did not even turn his head to answer his brother, but bent before Helen and said, "Shall we walk along the walls, lady? The view of the plain should look well in the moonlight. We shall see the river and Mount Ida."

But Helen shook her head. She said, "I shall go to my women and weave for a while. It is too cold a night for walking around the walls of this windswept heap of stones."

She got up and strode swiftly from the door. Asterius ran down the steps and met her before she reached her bower. She ruffled his hair and said, "Why, you are quite damp. You will get a cold, you silly boy. Come, we will see that you change into warm clothes. I do declare, you are a big fellow of nearly twelve, yet you cannot look after yourself, much less after my horses. At your age I and my sister Clytemnestra were already looking around Hellas for a husband."

4 Smintheus' Songs

The bower was very warm because the women there had drawn the leather curtains over the window holes and had built up fires in three large braziers. One of them warmed spiced wine in a bronze bowl and made Asterius drink it while Helen rubbed him down with a rough towel of linen and then made him put on a thick tunic of blue wool.

She took him to the padded bench by the biggest brazier and made him sit beside her and tease out some wool for her. Then, like a rather stern sister, she said, "You were up on the gallery, listening to the royal kindred. Do you deny it?"

Asterius shook his head. "No, lady," he said. "I was there. I came to bring you some news."

Helen said, "That can wait. Now listen to me—if you are ever caught eavesdropping in this dark prison, do you know what they will do to you?"

Asterius shook his head, smiling. He said, "If you

are here to look after me, they won't dare do anything, my lady."

Suddenly Helen seemed about to slap him. But
she drew her hand back and said, "Kings dare do
what they choose, slave. Whether they are Trojans
or Greeks. Never forget that. Besides, I may not always be here to protect you. Think about that. I
might go away, back to Sparta."

Then she signaled to a young slave girl who sat in
the corner holding a turtle-shell lyre, and the girl began to strum on the strings and to sing a sad song
about Sparta. To hear her, one would have thought
that Sparta was the most beautiful place on earth,
and that the folk there were the kindest. But Asterius
had heard different things, and anyway he knew
the poet who had made that song up. It was a man
called Smintheus, the Mousy One, who had never
been within two hundred miles of Sparta and who
couldn't have spoken the language if he had been
there.

Helen said sharply, "What was your news, then,
eavesdropper?"

Asterius said, "I shall only tell you if you promise
not to go away from Troy and leave me here."

Then Helen got up and paced around the room
awhile, swishing her skirts and frowning. At last she

sat down again and said, "I do not know why I put up with you. Very well, I promise. Now tell me your news."

He said, "Among the Greeks there is a king called Odysseus and another called Palamedes."

Helen gave a sharp tug at his ear and said, "Well, is that all? I know both of them, better than I know you, slave."

Asterius said, "Well, you only know one of them now, because Odysseus had the other one killed to-night. I saw them stone him for being a traitor—but he wasn't. It was Odysseus who put the gold in the other king's tent."

Helen held her hand up to her mouth and said at last, "So, the Greeks are beginning to kill each other now. If we only wait long enough, we shall have no need to follow Paris' plan, or to pray to the gods, or anything. They will destroy themselves."

Then she turned on Asterius and this time gave him quite a hard slap. "You have been outside the walls," she said. "Why, you silly fellow, don't you know that someone might have put an arrow into you? Is that all you think of me, to go risking your stupid life down there among the savage beasts? I should have you thrashed. I should have you thrown into a deep dungeon."

But instead she put her arms around him and

hugged him to her. Asterius thought how strange these grown-ups were. He said, "No, let me go, Helen. I want to tell you . . ."

But she still held him close and said, "You can't tell me anything about Odysseus that I don't know, you goose. Even the foxes go to that king of Ithaca for advice. Now be still and listen to the girl playing the lyre."

He listened to the other songs by Smintheus, about Sparta and brave warriors, and what it was like to drive in a great chariot among the whistling arrows. And at last he said, "I do not like this music, Helen. It is all lies. Smintheus is a little man with mouse-colored hair. He would not face up to a full-grown cat, much less a Spartan. He is not a hero, like Hector."

Helen looked at him very closely then and said, "Do you like Hector, my little stable-slave?"

Asterius nodded. "If I can only grow as big as he is," he said, "I shall be a hero like Hector."

Helen smiled sadly and said, "You Thracians do not grow to that size, my love. Besides, there is nothing in all this boasting and sword-clashing. All these heroes die. The sword takes them all. It will take Agamemnon even, one day. Then who will remember him but the small mouse-haired ones like Smintheus? Is that the fame you desire?"

Asterius put on his hardest face. "It will not take Hector," he said. "He is made in the model of Zeus."

Helen drew away from him a little and sucked in her breath. The lyre player stopped sounding the strings; the women at the looms held their hands where they were.

Helen said quite coldly, "If you compare a man with the god again in my hearing, I must have you killed. You must not forget that. I love you, but I must have you killed."

Asterius felt a shiver go up and down his back. He was afraid now that he had dared to call his mistress by her name, only a few moments before. But he spoke out and said, "Very well, lady, but I still say that Hector is the nearest man has grown to becoming like the god."

Helen of Troy sat very still then, like an image made of ice. Her nostrils pulled themselves in very tight and she spoke in a thin voice. She said, "You may say that. That might not offend the Furies, if you are lucky tonight, and I think you are. But you are wrong; Hector is not the greatest of them all, fine as he seems. Achilles is the greatest—though he sulks in his tent and chooses not to fight. If Hector challenges him the wrong way, then you will see if Hector is a god or not. Now go to bed."

The room had grown so cold, Asterius got up

straightway and went to his bed. No one in that bower spoke, as he went through the room, to wish him good night or to tease him. That made it worse than ever.

5 Cunning Odysseus

There were some cold weeks then. Wolves came up the stony slopes of Troy, right to the Scaean Gate, and howled. People threw rocks and hot water down onto them and laughed when they ran toward the Greek stockade. The Hittites came in when the weather improved, standing upright in their chariots, jingling in bronze and gold and led by a proud king called Dudkhalia. They were all small dark men with hawk faces and high conical helmets. Even in the cold blast of the plains they wore nothing on their upper bodies except long brown cloaks. Asterius saw their strange axes and curved swords, their

chain-mail kilts and the long horsetails they wore at the back of their helmets, reaching down to the waist. They would not talk to anyone lower than Hector or Priam. He heard them speaking once in the great hall, and their words were like the growling of bears, he thought. He wondered if such folk ever smiled or sang happy songs.

With them they brought a woman warrior called Penthesilea. She was not of their folk, being almost so yellow-haired as to be silver, but she dressed as they did and drove her chariot at the head of a thousand girl archers, who had their own silver totem, signifying the crescent moon.

"Who are these strange folk?" Asterius asked Helen as they stood on the balcony watching the warriors come in. Helen said with a smile, "You may well ask, boy. They call themselves Amazons and profess to come from Snowland. I can tell you no more, but I must command you not to go down into their encampment. They have strange customs and I am not sure that I could get you out of trouble if you offended them in any way."

She liked the Hittites though, and said what proper men they would be, if only they stood a little taller. Asterius did not like any of them. They were so different from anything he had seen before.

From this time he tried to stay as close to Hector

as he could and trailed him about the palace and the city, even when he was talking busily with his brother Paris or his second-in-command, Aeneas.

One day Hector noticed him and, sending the other two away for a moment, beckoned Asterius to come to him.

"What do you want, slave?" the hero said, smiling through his short copper-colored beard.

Asterius said, "I want nothing, my lord. Only to look at you."

Hector frowned and said, "Helen has told me a thing or two, my boy. Now let me tell you something of value—get rid of this dream of heroes as soon as you can. Be your own hero. That is all."

Asterius bowed and said, "Sir, forgive me, you are the hero. I am a slave. I have seen you about the city; all men are your friends, all respect you, you have no enemies."

Hector looked over his head, then said, "I have exactly as many enemies as I have friends, lad. And they are the same people. There is not a street sweeper in Troy who would not put the spear through me if he could—not because he hates me for myself, but because he too dreams of becoming a hero like me—better than me. Go back to your stable, boy, and rub the horse Hippomedon down. That is more useful than being a hero."

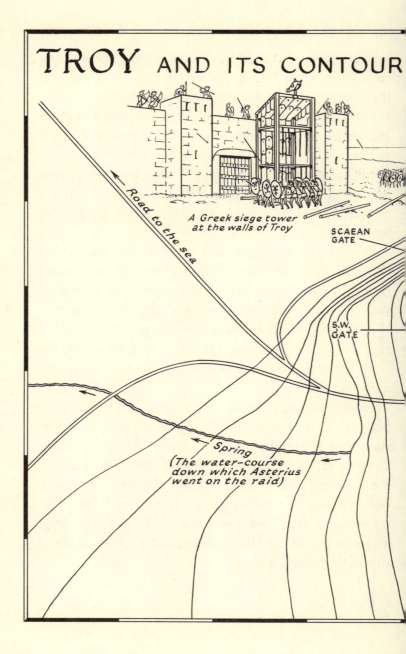

TROY AND ITS CONTOUR

Road to the sea

A Greek siege tower
at the walls of Troy

SCAEAN
GATE

S.W.
GATE

Spring
(The water-course
down which Asterius
went on the raid)

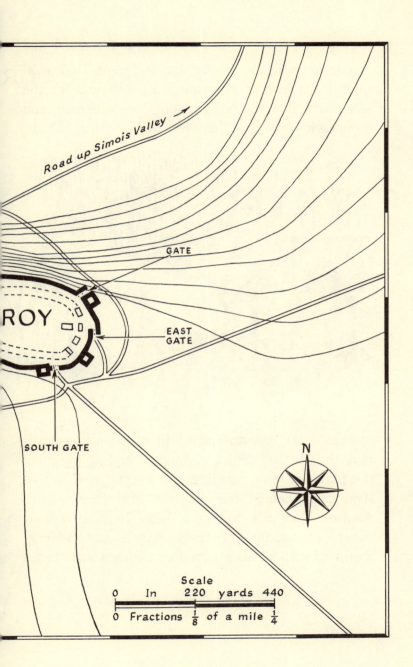

Road up Simois Valley

GATE

ROY

EAST
GATE

SOUTH GATE

N

Scale

0   In   220 yards 440

0 Fractions ⅛ of a mile ¼

Asterius went away after that and wept. He leaned against the hay in Hippomedon's stall and let the salt tears flow down. Hippomedon whinnied and stamped his hoof, but there was little comfort in that.

Then later Asterius heard from the other slaves that the Hittites had done pretty well at sweeping the plain clear of foraging Greeks and had shoved them back behind the stockade. But Penthesilea's Amazons had not had such luck. In one of their sweeps against the hide tents, Achilles had suddenly appeared with all his Myrmidons and had surrounded them. Some said that Achilles had struck down the Amazon queen and had dragged her body by the foot to the shore before flinging it into the water for the fishes.

Asterius asked, "This Achilles, is he such a god? I thought he stayed in his tent sulking because he had been offended by the Greek king."

The slave he spoke to, a brown-eyed boy from Tenedos, said, "Achilles Thin Mouth has no master. He was born sulking because there are gods above men. Soon you will see what this sulking leads to, when he comes for Hector."

Asterius said in astonishment, "So, has he accepted Hector's challenge at last?"

The slave from Tenedos laughed in the new sunshine and said, "Achilles ignores all challenges. He is above them. Hector has got him to fight by that sort of challenge which is not put into words. Hector has shot an arrow into Achilles' dearest friend, Patroclus. They will meet below the city, with the armies standing well clear, tomorrow or the next day. And after that perhaps I will not be a slave, but will go back to Tenedos."

Asterius said, "Why should that be? Have you saved up your freedom price?"

The boy laughed and shook his head. "No," he

said, "but after tomorrow there may be no Troy.
Achilles may decide to capture it."

It was dusk when this was said, so Asterius hur-
ried home to tell his mistress. The great palace was
silent, the slaves were in their own quarters chattering by the fires, and the corridor guards were in the
Mess, eating.

Asterius burst into Helen's bower and cried out,
"Lady, lady, they are going to fight after all. Hector
will kill their sulking brute."

Then he was aware that Helen was not alone in
the dimly lit bower. She sat by the brazier together
with a man, whose dark gray hood was over his head.
The slave women had been sent away and the looms
and the lyre stood unused.

Helen spoke first and said, "Do you not knock before you enter my bower, slave?"

Asterius was about to say how sorry he was when he saw that she was teasing him. Then suddenly the man drew his hood back and Asterius saw that Odysseus sat there in the charcoal glow. He almost fell to the floor in fear, but the Greek just nodded at him lightly and said with a crooked smile, "It has been a long time since we first met, lad, under that laurel bush—the night we had to put poor Palamedes out of the way."

Asterius gasped. "I did not know you had seen me, lord," he said.

Odysseus shrugged his massive shoulder and stirred the hot charcoal with his thick forefinger. He said, "I almost put my sword into you, boy. I thought it was a wolf skulking under there, at first. Anyway, I'm glad I didn't because you showed me the secret way up the pipe into the city. So, I'm grateful to you. Here, take this cloak pin as my gift."

Asterius drew away from the big brown hand and said, "If I called the guard, they would kill you. The Trojans would like to know that a Greek was inside the city."

Odysseus nodded and smiled. "If you called the guard," he said, "I should first have to kill you and then your mistress. I have my dagger here, under this cloak. So let us not talk any more foolishness."

Helen rose and took Asterius by the hand. "The King of Ithaca has come in kindness," she said. "Try to remember your manners, Asterius. He offers me a safe passage back to Sparta when Troy falls, and he brings me a loving message from my husband, Menelaus. You and I could leave tonight, with Odysseus, down the pipe. How does that suit you?"

Asterius said, "Lady, how could I leave Troy? Hector fights tomorrow and will free us from the Greeks forever."

The King of Ithaca poked his finger into his hairy ear and smiled. Then, in a deep rumbling voice he said, "Troy will never be free of Greeks, my lad. Not now, after ten years of our raiding. We do not give up like that. We need a passage up the Hellespont, to the goldfields there. As for this Hector of yours, someone should warn him not to set foot outside tomorrow, for if he does, it could be the end of him."

Asterius felt the blood rising in his face. He turned on the King of Ithaca and said, "You were the traitor, not Palamedes. I will tell Hector you are here. He will know how to deal with you."

He ran from the bower and no one stopped him. Outside the armory, where Hector was usually to be found when he was not in the Mess with the soldiers, he slowed down and got his breath again. He knocked three times on the thick oak door and heard Hector give him leave to enter.

Hector sat on an oak sword-chest talking to Paris and Aeneas. They all wore their war gear and were drinking deep-red wine out of shallow, glazed cups of Minyanware.

Hector glanced at him and nodded, then went on with what he had been saying. "I have a plan, you see, brother. He is much stronger in the arm than I am, though weaker in the leg. So I shall first take the force out of his legs, and then turn and try his arm. You will see, it will work. Then, once he is down, his Myrmidon army will go back home. They will not fight under anyone but Achilles. After that—Agamemnon will be nothing."

Asterius cried out, "Odysseus is in the palace. He is trying to take the lady Helen away, my lord."

He thought that they would jump up and shout or do something. But the three of them just looked at him blankly, and at last Paris said, "Off you go to bed, Asterius. You are very tired and I think you have a cold coming on. That is because you have been up on the walls too long today, watching those Amazons!"

Asterius ran to Hector and said, "But, sir, you could catch him if you came now. He is in the bower and only has a dagger."

Then Hector gazed at him so hard that Asterius was ashamed and turned and went back through the tall oak door without saying any more.

He met Helen on the way to the slaves dormitory. She was singing gaily and stopped a moment to say, "Not in bed yet, Asterius?"

He said sullenly, "Where is that traitor Odysseus, lady?"

She made lines in her forehead as though thinking, then said with a smile, "Odysseus? That old fox? Why, in his tent behind the stockade, I expect. Did you think you had seen him, my love? You must have been dreaming, as usual! I really must get a new horseboy—one who does not dream so much."

6 Achilles' Wrath

Fighting began early the next morning. Asterius stood beside Helen above the great limestone Scaean Gate, looking down toward the stony plain below the walls toward the river Scamander. Crowds lined the walls in grim silence. King Priam stood with his old counselors in their dark robes. Queen Hecabe, among her women, had covered her gray head with a black cloth and stood quietly praying to Zeus and Aphrodite for peace.

Helen whispered to Asterius, "More than prayers will be needed today, I think." She was smiling strangely as she spoke. Then suddenly the skirmish-

ing below the walls seemed to stop, and the two armies drew back from one another, leaving an open
space between them. Many of the Trojans came up
through the gates and took their helmets off as
though the war were over, as though there were nothing to worry about.

Then without warning old King Priam shouted
out, "I beg you, Hector, do not fight this savage
beast. Have pity on me. Come inside the walls, my
son."

He had hardly finished when Queen Hecabe cried
out, tears running down her cheeks, "Think of your
mother, Hector, and do not meet that monster in
single combat. Take your friends Paris and Aeneas
with you."

The crowds began to mutter, half-ashamed at
these words. Helen whispered, "They were not wise
to call down at him like that. Such words could un-
nerve a man. See, Hector is dragging his feet now.
He has lost his pride. He is sorry he killed Patroclus
now, I think."

Asterius stretched up to look over the balustrade.
First he saw tall Achilles, standing in a dusty open
space, looking like a giant in his crested helmet, with
the morning sunlight glinting on his bronze armor
and his blue cloak floating out behind him. Over his
right shoulder he carried a long, ash-shafted spear,

on his left arm a long leather shield with a lion's head painted on it. He seemed to be laughing, but the noise that came out of his closed helmet was like a bull roaring.

Hector heard this and stood still. His own long shield, marked with the sign of a flying bird, suddenly seemed to tremble, and almost fell from his arm. The crowd on the walls groaned and Queen Hecabe suddenly shrieked out as though she had seen a vision. Down below Hector seemed to hear his mother, for he glanced upward toward where she stood. Then all at once he swung around and began to run, as though to come inside the gates. Men rushed to withdraw the bars and get the doors open for him. Achilles stared in amazement for an instant, then, howling like a wolf, rushed after him. Dust spurted from Achilles' feet as he plunged forward. Helen said quietly, "Well may Hector have a dove on his shield—see how he flies!"

But Hector did not make for the gate now; swinging suddenly, he began to race around the base of the walls, past the lookout tower and a windswept fig tree, then along a narrow cart track. Achilles, hampered by his great cloak, was twenty paces behind. A cloud of gray dust followed them. Asterius, now leaning over the wall, saw them plunge almost waist-deep into the two springs that flowed down to the river Scamander. Helen said, "See, Achilles is drawing up to him. We shall not see Hector again."

Then the two plunged through a broad stone trough where the women of Troy usually knelt to do their washing, and were lost to view. Soon, from farther around the wall, a man shouted out, "Hector is making for the Dardanian Gate. Swing it open for him, some of you. Hey, you bowmen, give him covering fire while he darts through."

But another man cried out, "It cannot be done. The Greek is right under the wall, we cannot get our bows far enough over to aim at him."

Then some women began to wail, "Zeus has failed us. Apollo has failed us. Achilles has headed Hector off from the gate. They are coming around again."

Three times Asterius saw the men pass below, each time splashing through the streams. He shut his eyes now and leaned his forehead against the cold limestone wall in misery.

Then all at once a great shout went up, "Look! Look! Hector has stopped and is facing the Greek at last! This is our hero!"

Asterius opened his eyes. He saw that Hector was less than ten spears' lengths from Achilles and was standing at bay, his left foot forward.

He heard Hector's cool voice, saying, "Now we shall see whose gods are the stronger, Greek. Only

one request—if you do have the luck to kill me, I
ask you to give up my body for decent burning by
my own people. I will do the same for you. Do you
agree?"

Then Achilles roared, "The wolf does not make
bargains with the lamb, Trojan. I see that you are
wearing the breastplate of my dear friend Patroclus.
You shall not wear it long. Nay, that you shall not!"

As he spoke, without any warning he flung his
long spear. Hector saw it in time and swayed away.
The spear stuck deep into the ground and as Achilles
raced to drag it out, Hector flung his own spear. It

was a perfect cast, but the Greek swung his shield up just in time and the weapon skittered away off the rounded surface, well out of reach.

Hector glanced back at the Trojans beneath the walls. "Throw me another spear, one of you!" he shouted. "Where is my friend Deiphobus? Can he not spare me his javelin? One of you! Any sort of spear!"

But Achilles was coming on too fast now with his long spear, and Hector had to move away. As he went he drew his sword, then jumped around to take his stance again. But his movement was so fierce that as he turned, his left ankle gave under him and he tottered off-balance for a moment. And in that moment Achilles' spearpoint entered the side of his neck, between the lower flap of his helmet and the throat ring of his armor. A sigh went up from the women on the walls, a great roar from the watching Greek warriors in their massed chariots. Hector stood for a while as though he could not believe what had happened; then, trying to pull out the spear, he slowly knelt in the dust and, looking up slowly at Achilles, said in a hoarse voice, "Do not throw me to the dogs."

Achilles stood over him, snarling like a hound himself. "I shall do worse than that, murderer of my friend," he said coldly.

Hector fell onto his hands. He seemed to shrug his shoulders then. On the walls they heard him say, "I can see I have been wasting my breath." Then he sank with his face in the dust and lay still.

The Trojans on the walls were dumbstruck as the Greeks ran forward and clustered around the still body. Many of them began to poke or slash down at Hector, but Achilles pushed them away roughly and began to tear off the Trojan's helmet and breastplate, howling all the while.

Helen put her arms around Asterius and said in a broken voice, "Let us go away, little one. I am sorry we saw it. There is no glory in it."

But Asterius pulled back and said, "Hector was my friend. If I were big enough I would go down to this brute Achilles. He is a beast."

Helen shook her head. "That is the duty of his brother Paris," she said sadly. "You are not of Hector's kin; you are a slave, my love."

Then she went away, helping to guide Queen Hecabe back to the palace. All the women were wailing now, and from the top step of the great hall Cassandra was shrieking out, "I foretold this, I foretold this. When will you fools of Troy believe me when I speak?"

King Priam was leaning on the arm of one of his counselors. He was looking down at the pavement and saying, "He must have a hero's funeral pyre. I shall go tonight down to their stockade and buy his poor body back, even if it costs all the gold in Troy to get it."

Asterius stayed there after the king had gone. He felt that it would be deserting Hector if he left before it was all over. He saw Achilles bend and slit the tendons behind Hector's feet, then thread leather thongs through them and tie them to the tail-board of his chariot. Shouting like a madman, the

Greek then whipped up his horses and dragged the warrior's body three times around the walls, along the cart track, over the streams, and through the water trough. Hector's dark hair trailed in the dust and the water. And when at last Achilles drove the chariot away toward the stockade, Asterius saw with horror that Hector, his hero, now looked no more human than a sack of meal, torn and dirtied with mud.

He went to the stables and told the horse Hippomedon about it all, then lay in the straw and cried himself to sleep.

7 Helen's Taunt

A deep gloom lay over Troy. It was like living in a nightmare. Each evening Asterius went to the walls and looked toward the wine-dark sea, where the Greeks lit their red fires, and shook his fist. Each night he dreamed of what he had seen below the walls. He wanted to tell Helen about it, but she had shut herself in her bower and would not see him. Prince Paris now roamed the dark palace like a glowering pale ghost, muttering to himself, and no one dared go near him. Women gathered at all the shrines, ashes on their heads, their robes now tattered and dirty, making offerings to the gods that

sent up whorls of black smoke from every altar fire.
Many of the Hittites began to lose patience in the
war and went off home in companies by night. Ru-
mors were going around that Cassandra had been
right after all, that Troy was doomed, and that it
was only a matter of time before the Greeks broke

in and set fire to the city. Some folk even said that
King Priam had left Troy and would never return.

But one morning the king came through the gates,
leading a mule-drawn cart on which lay Hector's
body. Cassandra led the Trojan women to greet
the dead hero. They brought musicians with them

and so the procession came to the palace steps. And there Priam stood above the people and cried out, "What is done is done, my friends. I have met Achilles and now I see him to be a great and god-like hero. He has let us have back the body of our prince and gives us permission to go out from Troy to gather wood for the funeral pyre. He has agreed to cease all warfare until Hector is laid to rest. So, for nine days we shall mourn him. On the tenth we shall bury him and hold our funeral feast. On the eleventh day we shall build him a mound. And the next day we must be ready to take up the sword once more."

Paris suddenly cried out, "I am ready now and my first revenge shall be on this brute Achilles."

Helen, standing beside him, put her hand over his mouth. "Think of Hector, not of Achilles," she said. "Dear Hector, he was the only true friend I ever had in Troy. The people here shudder at me as I pass, but Hector never spoke a harsh word to me."

Paris turned from her in anger and went away. Asterius tried to speak to her, but she did not notice him.

Then for nine days the men went outside the city, chopping down trees and bringing the wood back on wagons. The Greeks did not ambush them. On the tenth day crowds flocked to see Hector's body car-

ried by his brothers and comrades to the top of a
great funeral pyre and stood, lamenting all night,
while the fierce flames licked around it, fed by the
fat of sheep and cattle. In the morning, at dawn, the
flames were quenched with wine and the hero's bones
were wrapped in purple cloth and placed inside a
golden urn. And, when this was lowered into a grave,
the Trojans first covered it with big stones and then
built a high mound of earth over it.

When the last spadeful was thrown on the mound,
Paris turned around to his cousin Aeneas and said,
"The time of peace is over now, my friend. From
this time forth I shall not sleep until Achilles lies
under my foot and breathes his last into the dust."

Asterius stood close to Paris when he said this, and
for a moment it was like looking into the face of a
wild creature, not a man. Almost before he had realized what he was saying, Asterius stepped forward
and touched the hem of the prince's tunic. "My
lord," he said, "let me come with you. I loved Hector too, although I am only a Thracian slave."

Paris did not hear him and brushed past, but thin-
faced, brown Aeneas paused in passing and said in a
soft voice, "You can run at the back of the raiding
party, if you can find yourself a weapon of some
sort."

Asterius flew to the smithy behind the stables.

There an old man named Talos was bent over an anvil hammering at a bronze wheel-rim. The boy went to him and said, "Talos, is there an old spear

I can borrow? I have made a bet with one of the other boys that I can throw farther than he can."

The old man wiped his hand over his streaming brow, then down his leather apron. So with a scornful movement of the head he indicated a heap of spoiled bronze that lay behind him. He did not even bother to see what Asterius chose. It was an old

socketed axe, cracked along one side, but still firm
in its curved shaft of ash. A good hand had once held
it and had made the shaft gleam.

Asterius was just in time to run at the end of the
column of warriors and youths, before the high gates
closed behind them. A crested guard who stood with
the bar in his hand called out, "Hey, does Helen
know where her pet is off to?" The other guards
laughed, but Asterius shut his ears to them and ran
on down the rocky slope toward the river.

The whole raid seemed unreal. The sun was shin-
ing brightly and cicadas were shrilling as they passed
a few peasants leading cows across the flowery plain
toward the river. These men wore broad-brimmed
straw hats and were fanning the black flies away
from the cattle with fronds of palm. They did not
even look up as the raiders ran past them. Asterius
felt that there should have been thick crowds of
folk along the walls and bronze trumpets blowing.
It was like running in a dream, when your feet do
not touch the ground. After a time he began to feel
very brave, seeing the men in front of him with
spears and bows. A youth who ran by his side carried a copper kitchen-spit as though it were a sword.
He had a long gash down one side of his face and
would not deign to speak to Asterius, although the
boy knew that this youth was a slave also, named

Nycteus, and he worked in the palace granary, stacking corn.

They went down into a green stream-bed suddenly and ran bent double for a while, with the frogs croaking about them. When they came up again, the Greek stockade lay only four hundred paces off and fires were still smoldering from the burial mounds behind it. You could smell the salt of the sea.

Asterius wondered why there were no Greeks about. Then suddenly he saw them climbing over the oak fence, dragging on their helmets, some of them with daggers held in their teeth. He could even see the beads of sweat on their bearded faces, and then he almost had to stop and be sick with fright.

Nycteus spoke to him for the first time and said, "Keep close to me, slave. And watch what you are doing with that old axe. I don't want any of my wounds to be at the back."

Up at the front there was a lot of noise and men swaying about all ways at once. Asterius wondered where Paris and Aeneas were, but just then a Greek came around a heap of straw at them, pulling on his leather corselet, his sword shoved into his belt. He had a stubbly red beard and big teeth; the language he was shouting meant nothing to Asterius. The slave Nycteus ran straight at this man, kicked his feet from under him, and stuck the kitchen spit up

under the corselet before the man could get it on.
"Quick," he shouted to Asterius, "hit him on the
head, he is still alive. See, he is breathing."

But Asterius could not bring himself to do it. He
felt Nycteus snatch the bronze axe from him, then
he looked away. On its hill Troy looked a long way
off. There was smoke rising from it and a gray mist
swirling around the lower slopes of rock.

Then all at once a man shouted out, "Back, lads,
back! They are all coming for us. We have stirred
up the hornets' nest!"

Nycteus shook Asterius by the hair and shouted
in his ear, "Run, you fool! Forget everything and
run."

Asterius forgot the dead Greek with the red beard
then and tried to keep up with the others. He thought
that it had not been a very heroic battle after all.
His breath was short and his heart thumped madly.
When they reached the green watercourse, most of
the Greeks left them and turned back, laughing, but
some kept coming on. Glancing over his shoulder
he saw that some of them wore tall helmets with
horse crests, but he did not know who they were. All
Greeks looked alike to him.

It seemed an age before he felt the sharp stones
of Troy Hill under his feet. His eyes were quite
misty with exhaustion, but he saw that Nycteus still

carried his cracked bronze axe, so he asked for it
back. But Nycteus was not listening. Instead he
pointed down the slope and gasped, "Look at that!
Why, Paris must have gone mad!"

And there, not fifty paces from where Hector had
taken his death thrust, Paris was kneeling in the
dust and drawing his bowstring back past his ear.
The arrowhead pointed upward, almost to the sun.

Far away a tall-crested Greek stood watching curiously, the last of the pursuers, his shadow long across the earth.

Nycteus just said, "What does he think he is doing?" Then the bowstring twanged and the arrow whirred away with a shrill buzzing. Asterius watched its arc at first, then he lost it, it sped so fast.

And suddenly the distant Greek dropped his long spear, flung up his arms, and cried out. Then his helmet fell off and he pitched forward, the arrow through both his legs just behind the ankle.

Aeneas clapped his thigh and shouted out, "Well, by Apollo, if I live to be a hundred I'll never see such a lucky shot as that again."

They were wondering whether to risk running back and stripping the man of his armor when another band of Greeks led by a massive, broad-shouldered warrior came up. Aeneas called out, "Back, lads. They are too many for us." So the raiding party went up and through the gate.

Asterius glanced down at the plain before the gates shut and saw the big Greek carrying the wounded one on his back. They were walking very slowly and the man with the arrow in his legs hung down like a sack of meal, all his limbs swinging loosely.

Toward evening, after Asterius had given old Talos the axe again, a woman came and said, "My lady Helen sends for you, slave. It would be best to hurry, she has already broken her loom with anger."

Helen was in the bower, tight-lipped and furious. The boy had never seen her so angry before. She said to him immediately, "Are you so anxious to die, fellow?"

Asterius knew that it was no use trying to hide anything from her. He knelt down before her and touched the hem of her robe with his lips. He whispered, "I am sorry, my lady."

Suddenly she shot out her foot and kicked him as he knelt. "Sorry," she stormed. "Sorry! You could be like Achilles now, stone dead from a chance arrow."

Asterius forgot the kick and stood up. "Achilles dead?" he said, bewildered. "How can he be dead? It was only a little raid. It was not a real battle."

Helen shouted, "Do you call me a liar, slave? I tell you that with his one arrow Paris shot Achilles dead this afternoon. And Ajax, Achilles' dearest friend, has gone mad with grief and has fallen onto his sword. You could have lain as stark as both of them by now, with your foolishness. I have loved you like my own child. You have replaced my own child, Hermione, in my heart."

He did not know what to say, he was so glad and so sad, both at the same time. He heard Helen say,

"And where did you get the weapon you took with you? Answer me straightway. I must know."

"From old Talos," he said. "But it was not his fault. I stole it while he wasn't looking. He did not know a thing about it. I am entirely to blame, lady."

"Very well," said Helen, "then go back to Talos and tell him to give you ten strokes with the birch for your wickedness."

Asterius went to Talos, walking in a dream, and told him what the punishment was to be. Old Talos wiped his brow and tucked up his apron. "Oh, aye," he said, feeling under the bench for his birch.

He did not lay on very hard after the first one and Asterius said, "Did you hear, Talos? Achilles is dead."

The blacksmith paused and wiped his brow again. "Oh, aye," he said. "That's only to be expected. They mostly die. How many strokes have we got up to, lad?"

Asterius said, "About five. I've lost count. Hey, and Ajax has fallen on his sword in grief. Did you hear that?"

Talos said, "For the love of Zeus, keep still. That Ajax was always a madman. It was only to be expected. Now go back and tell the lady that I have carried out her orders."

He sat down, grumbling again, and Asterius went back whistling to the bower. Paris was sitting with Helen now, punching one fist against the other excitedly. "This is an omen," he was saying. "Tomorrow I shall go to them again. While the luck is with me. Whom shall I kill this time? Tell me and I will do it."

Helen said wearily, "I am sick of this killing. I am sick of Troy. I am sick of you, Paris, if you must know. I want to be away."

But he did not seem to hear her and kept saying, "Name anyone you please. Name Agamemnon, name Menelaus. Name anyone."

Then Helen said in a distant voice, "Very well, go to the Greeks and kill their most famous archer. Kill Philoctetes if you must kill someone. There would be some honor in that, Paris. But I doubt if you are the man to do it."

Paris began to rave so loudly then that Asterius crept away. He thought that Helen would be in no mood to talk to him anymore that day.

8 Oak Grove

There was no fighting for many days now. Shepherds who came into Troy from the hills south of the Scamander said they had seen many black Greek ships, some of them setting course toward Tenedos and Lemnos, others driving down south toward Lesbos.

Asterius stood with old Talos in the yard and said, "Is the war over, do you think? Now that their chieftains Achilles and Ajax are dead, have the Greeks decided to go away again?"

Talos was knocking a rivet into a sword handle and did not look up. "They will never go away," he said. "You cannot trust shepherds. They spend so much time alone, high on the hills, with only their sheep to talk to, they live in a world of dreams. If the Greeks have sailed, then it is either to raid the islands for food, or to take their dead kings to some sacred place for burial. They will come back, you can be sure of that."

Then he went on with his riveting and forgot the boy and the Greeks. His work was more important to him than war and heroes.

The mourning for Hector had ended and the folk of Troy seemed to have forgotten they had ever been sad. Girls wore garlands of red flowers and danced to the shepherds' pipes, laughing, under the plane trees in the square; the soldiers stood about, with their helmets off, watching them and pointing and sipping wine; even the priestesses had washed the clay from their faces and had put on clean white gowns. Doves as gray and gleaming as pearls fluttered over the red-tiled houses in the sunshine. Only the great dark palace still mourned. King Priam and Queen Hecabe still wore their black robes and moved like shadows along the corridors of the great house. Sometimes at night Cassandra would cry out in her shrill voice, and the slaves would smile at one another and tap their foreheads.

Asterius hated to walk through the palace now, it

was so cold and dimly lit, full of dark corners and echoes. Once he saw Helen passing with her women at the end of a passageway, but she gazed ahead and did not call out to him. And once he heard a strange clanging in the Bull Court and crept along the wall

to see what was happening. It was Paris striking at the great monster with his sword and shouting out, "I will teach that Spartan woman to mock me! I will go at her famous Greek Philoctetes like this, and this, and this! I will make him pay for the death of my brother!"

And with each sentence he struck at the bronze bull, hacking his sword edge and filling the court with echoes right up to its dark rafters. Aeneas was leaning by a pillar with his hand on his chin, shaking his dark head. He kept saying, "Gently, cousin, gently. You will exhaust yourself and break your sword."

Asterius felt sure that Paris had gone mad. He knew that there was an ancient saying: "Whom the gods mean to destroy, they first make mad." So he crept away, out of that grim palace, into the bright sunlight, and went to the stable where Helen's lovely white horse Hippomedon stood flicking the flies away with his long tail. There was no one about, so Asterius put his arm around Hippomedon's neck and rubbed his face against the horse's jawbone.

He whispered to the horse, "We are like prisoners here, you and I. The Greeks have kept us all penned up in his maze till we are going mad. Would you like to escape, Hippomedon?"

The white horse turned his dark eye around and looked at the boy, then he whinnied and seemed to nod his great head. Asterius slapped him on the neck gently and said, "So would I, dear friend. I think that Helen has forgotten all about us both. She never rides you and never talks to me. Would you like to gallop up along the river, toward Mount Ida? There

are no Greeks about, and I know a little grove where
we could splash in the water and keep cool, away
from this windy, dusty city. Would you like that,
brother?"

Hippomedon began to stamp his hoof as though
he were anxious to be off, so Asterius untied his hal-
ter and led him quietly behind the stables, then
down a narrow gully in the rock until they came to
one of the most ancient of the city's many walls. It
was all overgrown with straggling bushes which hid
its crumbling parts. On the other side there was a
newer wall, but if you went between the two walls,
heading eastward, you came at last to a rocky ledge,
and then down a steep slope and out of the city al-
together. Not many people knew about this place,
mainly old slaves, and they did not tell anyone because this was the way they used when they wished
for a little freedom at night. Hippomedon went as
surefooted as a goat. No one saw them and before
long they were down on the plain, cantering beside
the winding river with no one to stop them or tell
them what to do.

It was good to be in the open again, seeing clear
water and green grass and Mount Ida towering up
in the distance almost straight ahead. Asterius even
forgot that he was a slave and began to sing like a
lark.

In a little bend of the river lay the oak grove.
There, among the tall trees, a spring welled up from
the ground and made a pool deep enough to swim
in. The water was always cool because it was shel-

tered from the hot sun by overhanging boughs. Asterius slid off Hippomedon's back and led him to a
place where the horse could drink this clear water;
then, when he had tethered him, the boy turned and
jumped right into the middle of the pool, making a
great splash and sending a shoal of small fishes scat-
tering away into the reeds.

He couldn't really swim, but with one foot on the bottom he struck out and pretended he could cross the Hellespont if only he wished. It was a glorious feeling, with the cool water on his back, and the sighing green leaves above him. It was like being in a green palace, so fresh and free, with no stone walls or smoking altars, or kitchen women nagging if you didn't come immediately when they called. Asterius thought, "If I were a king, I would not live in a palace. I would have my house in a green grove like this one."

Then suddenly Hippomedon whinnied in fright, and at the same time Asterius heard a deep dry cough, like the sound a lion makes at night when he prowls around the sheeppens, looking for an open gate. Asterius almost jumped out of his skin. He swung around suddenly to where the sound came from and his heart seemed to stop beating.

Knee-deep among the reeds behind him stood a man. Or was it the god himself? Asterius had often heard that Zeus visited Mount Ida when he wished. Shepherds had seen him, tall and menacing on the hillside at dusk, they said. And this man was so tall, in his bronze helmet, that the stiff horsehair crest brushed against the overhanging boughs. Everything about him was menacing: his piercing gray eyes, that looked out above the cheekpieces, his arms

and legs as shaggy as a wolf, his leaf-shaped bronze sword, his terrible long spear. Asterius had never seen such broad shoulders, such a great chest that seemed to bulge the leather body-armor outward.

The boy prayed swiftly, "O Lady Aphrodite, come to my aid. I forgot to give you my knife that night under the laurel bush, but I swear I will offer it tomorrow if you will come quickly. Only come quickly, please."

The giant among the reeds listened to the boy, gazing hard at him, then suddenly he turned away and slung the great square shield off his back. It was of dark polished leather with a lion painted on it, rearing and roaring with its jaws open. He set the shield against an oak bole, put his weapons carefully beside it, then dragged off his helmet, making a groaning sound as it came away from his cheeks.

Then Asterius saw his red raw face, all criss-crossed with white scars. He saw the close-cropped dusty brown hair and the thick stubbly beard with gray in it that grew up to the giant's lower eyelids.

The man said suddenly, "Is the water cold? You are shivering."

Asterius tried to speak, but could not, so he just nodded.

The man said, "Then I shall not risk getting a cold. I thought I might bathe here. I am covered with dust from the plain. All this burning of villages, these funeral pyres, they make a man dusty." He smiled then and it was not very pleasant to see. A deep furrow along one side of his face, all white and puckered, dragged up his lip in a wolf snarl. Asterius began to edge away to the far side of the pool, but the man pointed his finger at him and said, "If you run away, I shall skewer you like a frog. Come out of that cold water and talk to me."

He held out the butt end of his spear for the boy to take hold of, then drew him to the reed-fringed shore. The man made his snarling smile again, then sat on a flat stone by the tree bole. He slapped the stone and said, "Sit here, beside me. There is room for us both."

In the warmth of the sun a strange smell came from the man; it was partly of unbleached linen, partly of sweaty leather. It was also the scent of dry hair. It was the warrior smell, Asterius thought.

Then the man said, "Did you see the emblem on my shield? Do you know who I am, boy?"

Asterius stared down at his feet and shook his head. The man said quietly, "I am the Lion of Mycenae, boy, the High King of Greece. I am Agamemnon. All the kings of Greece obey me."

Then he put his hard, dry hand on the boy's shoulders and said in a gentler voice, "You are shivering worse than ever. Have you heard of me before?"

Asterius nodded. His teeth began to chatter quite loudly. The man said, "You have been listening to old slave women, I can tell. They spread bad sto-

ries about kings. Do I look like an ogre, boy?" He took hold of Asterius' chin gently and turned his head around. "You must look at me when I speak to you. Do I look like an ogre?"

Asterius found he could only whisper. He said, "Yes, lord. I mean, no, lord. Oh, I don't know."

Agamemnon loosed him and smiled down at the pool. He said, "I do not eat up little boys. Though sometimes, when I am very hungry, I might eat up their fathers—if they are Trojans. But only if I am very hungry and there is no ox meat or sheep meat. I never eat fish, though. Do you eat fish?"

Asterius nodded dumbly. The man said, "Then you are either a Trojan or a slave. Which are you?"

Asterius said in a shaking voice, "I am Helen's slave, lord. But I am not a Trojan."

Agamemnon got up from the stone very slowly and seemed to grow up to the sky. Asterius shut his eyes and waited to be speared. But the man was reaching up and breaking twigs off a high branch. He said in a low voice, "Is your mistress happy, boy? She is a kinswoman of mine, but I have not seen her for years. Is she happy?"

Asterius shook his head. "I think she wants to go home to Sparta, lord," he said. "She hardly ever speaks to me now, but she used to play with me at one time."

Agamemnon looked at him keenly, then said, "I see she still lets you ride her horse. She cannot be so bad a mistress."

Then he began to kick at the reeds and said in a different voice, "Did they give Hector a good funeral? I heard he fought well, but had bad luck when he slipped and fell onto the spear. I did not watch it."

Asterius said, more boldly now, "He had a chieftain's burial mound. And his luck was no worse than Achilles', being caught by a chance arrow from so far away."

Agamemnon nodded. "Yes," he said, "it is mostly a matter of luck. The poets sing about bravery and cunning, and so on, but they have never held a spear. It's mostly luck, one way or the other. Would you like to be a soldier, lad?"

Asterius said, "No, lord. I once went on a raid, but I did not like it. I would not like to be a soldier, lord."

The Lion of Mycenae laughed a short laugh then and said, "You are one of the few honest men I have met, boy. I am the High King of all the warrior Greeks and cannot even count the battles I have been in. But I am still so afraid before a raid that I cannot keep food or drink down. Would you believe that?"

But before Asterius could answer, the High King went on, "Talking of food and drink, do you have enough to eat and drink up in that windy city now? My spies tell me that you go a bit short."

Asterius said, "We have good days and bad, like the rest of the world." Agamemnon glanced at him so sharply then that he felt he had said something wrong. But when the High King asked, "And how is

Paris? Is he raving and vowing vengeance on the Greeks?" Asterius clenched his jaws and would not answer.

Agamemnon nodded in approval. "You are not a bad fellow," he said. "I can tell that you can keep a secret. I like a man who can do that."

He walked about among the reeds for a while, letting the water come halfway up his legs and rubbing the palm of his right hand against his beard, making a bristly sound. At last he said, "Can you carry a message as well as you can keep a secret?"

Asterius pulled his tunic over his head and began to lace up his sandals. He nodded his head. "I expect so, lord," he said.

Agamemnon came back to the rock and knelt before the boy on the short turf. His face was smiling strangely. He leaned forward and whispered, "Then tell the lady Helen that she has not long to wait before she will see Sparta again. Just tell her that, she will understand. But tell no one else. Is that a promise?"

Asterius nodded. The High King felt in his pouch and drew out a cloak pin made of bright copper. He said, "This is your reward for carrying that message, boy."

But Asterius held his hands behind his back and

said, "My lord, I do not wish to be paid for taking a message to my mistress. That would make me feel like a dog that has to be given a piece of meat when it has sat up like a man or walked on its hind legs."

King Agamemnon stared at the boy for a while in astonishment. Then suddenly he smiled rather sadly and said, "It is easy to tell that you are not a Greek, my boy. But a king is brought up from the cradle to reward all who do him a service. It is an ancient law and I may not break it. So what I shall now give you is something of the greatest worth; you cannot refuse it, because it will pass from me to you too swiftly. And you cannot throw it away, once it has been given. You cannot even show it to anyone or wear it about your neck. It will lie forever in your deepest heart."

Asterius looked wide-eyed up at the king, but did not speak.

Then great Agamemnon leaned on the oak bole and said in his deep hoarse voice, "I came to this grove to pray to your quick-minded god Apollo for guidance in what I should do to take Troy. I did not expect that he would tell me, but I hoped that he might forget himself for an instant and give me a hint. While I have been talking to you, the god has whispered in my head and I know what to do."

Asterius clapped his hands over his ears, but Agamemnon gently took them away and said, "From the tall trees of this grove I shall have made a tower. It shall have rollers at its base so that oxen can drag it up to Troy. On the outside it shall have dampened horsehides, so that the Trojans cannot set fire to it. This tower shall stand so high that the men who go

up inside it can climb over into the city. And, in mockery of Hector the Horse Tamer, as he was nicknamed, I will set a horse's head on my tower."

Asterius jumped up from the stone and ran to

where Hippomedon was pawing at the turf, tired of waiting. He called back, "What if I tell this to King Priam?"

But Agamemnon was pulling on his helmet and only laughed. "He is too far gone in grief, my lad," he said. "And the others would say you were mad. I think you will keep my secret. But be sure that you give my message to your mistress."

Hippomedon was glad to be away again, and so was Asterius. Until he was clear of the wood with its overhanging boughs, he felt an itching spot in the middle of his back, where a spear might have struck if some great warrior had cast it.

But Agamemnon had already forgotten about the boy and was whistling through the grove, planning his tower. And Asterius soon forgot Agamemnon, because when he got back into the city at dusk, he heard a great wailing and the deep lowing of bronze horns.

Old Talos was hammering bronze in the yard, and Asterius said to him, "What is all the noise for, Talos? What has happened?"

The smith put down his pincers and hammer and blew out his stubbly cheeks, then wiped his forehead with his apron. "Happened?" he said. "Why, what always happens, lad, when princes go seeking what they call revenge."

Asterius leaned against the anvil and forgot that it was still quite hot. He said, "Is it Paris, old Talos?"

The smith nodded and picked up a piece of bronze to look at it. "Aye," he said evenly, "it is Paris. He

went looking for some Greek or another, and came back with arrows through his right arm, his leg, and his eye. It was the last one that finished him. They brought him up the hill on a cloak with four men carrying it. Now only Aeneas is left. I shall be glad when he has gone as well; then I can go back to my proper trade of wheelwright, instead of all this sword-hammering and spear-hammering."

Asterius went to the slaves' dormitory with the sound of old Talos' hammer in his ears—that and the memory of Paris' beating at the bronze bull earlier that day, filling the dark palace with its mad clangor. He had forgotten all else—even great Agamemnon in the wood, even the message for Helen, even the strange wooden tower. He was so full of sadness for poor mad Paris, it filled all his dreams.

9 Wooden Horse

Just after dawn the following morning Asterius woke to hear the slaves all around him shouting, "They have gone! The Greeks have gone!"

He rolled out of his hard straw bed and went to the nearest window hole. Between two sloping roofs he could see a small stretch of the distant shore where they had once camped behind the oak stockade. Now, between the roofs, he saw clouds of gray smoke swirling thickly in the sea breezes. A great Libyan slave smiled at him and said, "They have fired their camp and sailed away. We shall be able to go hunting again along the river, boy." Asterius nodded to him and the man went off, laughing and showing his white teeth.

He washed carefully and put on his neatest tunic, a pale red one, and some sandals of untanned calfskin that looked white and clean. He thought he would report to Helen's bower and see what duties she might have for him that day, but just as he was oiling and combing his long hair, a slave master leaned around the door and shouted out, "All you slaves! Stop chattering and listen. The Greeks have gone away and Troy is free again. King Priam has declared a feast day for all the warriors and free folk. He and his queen will mourn dead Paris, but he gives all others leave to feast."

The slaves began to cheer until the master said in a stern voice, "You are not warriors, neither are you free folk. You have no cause for cheering. You will serve at the tables today and tonight, and for as long as our king decrees."

So Asterius took off his best red tunic and white sandals and, instead, put on a jerkin of soiled leather and some light shoes with cork soles. Then he went down to the courtyard where the cooks were assembled, together with the vintners and meat carvers, and awaited his orders from the score of chamberlains.

By midday his fingers were so burned from car-

rying hot dishes and his feet so raw from running
from room to room, he could have wept. By dusk he
was so weary that he had no strength left to weep.
And at last he stepped over the warriors who lay
snoring in the straw of the great hall and dragged
himself back up the stairs to the slaves' dormitory.
He yawned and said to himself, "If this is freedom,
what is slavery? If this is victory, what is defeat?"

On the way up he passed old Talos, still wiping
his brow with his leather apron. The smith was carrying a hammer in one hand and a pair of pincers in
the other. As they drew alongside, Talos winked and
whispered, "As one slave to another, a word of good
advice, lad. Always carry something around in your
hands, some tool of the trade; then no one will ever
set you to laying tables and serving. Remember that
—you look worn out."

Asterius thanked him and almost fell backward
down the stairs. Then he went to his bed, smiling at
what the old man had said, and was fast asleep before he even got his sandals off.

He was just in the middle of a dream where Hippomedon was his own horse, and they were gallop-
ing away to the sunrise, when someone shook him
and thumped him and shouted loudly in his ear,
"Get up, lad, get up, or you will burn in your bed!
The Greeks are back!"

All the slaves were running about crying, "The Greeks are back! O Apollo, the Greeks are back!"

Once more Asterius dragged himself to the window hole and looked out. This time he saw red flames, not swirling smoke, and the flames were much nearer than the smoke had been, at dawntime. He started to go down the stairs again, but the big Libyan took him by the shoulder and pulled him back. He was not laughing now. Instead he said, "Zeus! Zeus! But if you go that way you will be dead. Follow me, lad."

So Asterius followed him, among a crowd of others, by the gallery that ran above the dormitory, and then over a shaking wooden bridge. They passed across a flat roof and out into the open for a moment. Then they had to bend under a low doorway and so reached a circular tower with a staircase that ran around its sides. Breathless now, they scrambled up the shaking stairs and at last came out onto a platform that looked on one side down to the Scaean Gates, and on the other into the city square of Troy.

There Asterius sat down, chilled through by the winds that always swept across that hill, to watch the fall of Troy. Standing high on the broad ledge of rock outside the city wall, he saw the tower that the High King had spoken of. It was made of tall oaks with the bark still on them and only roughly

shaped. Thick boughs were lashed, crosswise, with leather thongs, to keep the structure rigid. It was square in shape, and the side which overlooked the top of the limestone wall was covered with wet hides, loosely nailed to the oak with thick bronze pins. Spears stuck in it but did not go through; arrows with flaming pitch on their points did not set fire to it, but bounced away harmlessly. At the summit of this tower was fixed the grinning mask of a horse, glistening white in the firelight. And at various stages of the tower Asterius saw platforms swarming with Greeks who leaned sideways to fling down their spears at the guards, or to shoot their own fire-arrows into the thatch of the houses underneath the wall, into the mazelike streets of Troy. From time to time he watched Greeks fall from these platforms, pierced by chance arrows, but always others swarmed up the ropes from below to take their places.

The great Libyan shook his head and said, "See, they have cleared the Trojans from the top of the wall, and now they are jumping down into the city. They are swarming over like ants. Soon they will unbar the gates from the inside to let the rest of their comrades through. It is not our war, we are slaves. We shall be safer up here. All who go down will be butchered." Then he turned away and went to comfort some young girls who were wailing with fear.

Asterius knew that the man was right and that now nothing could be done to save Troy. Down in the square he saw Aeneas, bareheaded and with his left arm bound in a stained cloth. He was trying to get the soldiers to go back to the wall, beating at them with the flat of his long sword; but they were running away and sweeping him along with them. Most of them had thrown down their spears. Some were crying.

Asterius knew then that not even great Hector or Paris could have put heart into the Trojans, who had already given up the fight and were rushing about like madmen, knowing they were trapped in the high-walled city. Then the Greeks came sweeping through in wave after wave, searching every street and alleyway, shouting like demons, showing no mercy. Asterius caught a glimpse of Agamemnon once, standing upright in a gold-painted chariot drawn by three horses. He seemed to be calling out to the men around him and looked angry; but no one was listening. Beside him in the chariot at his left stood a white-haired old man leaning on a stick and nodding his head; at his right stood crafty Odysseus, laughing and joking with the men as they flung lighted torches into the windows of the houses.

Then other chariots and floating banners went past,
and Asterius lost sight of the High King.

On the far side of the central city square there
was a little courtyard, with an old sacred laurel tree
in the middle, and under it an altar to Zeus. Here

Asterius saw Queen Hecabe standing with her arms
around old King Priam. So far the Greeks had raced
past this place without noticing it, and Asterius
hoped that the two old people would keep quiet. But
just then a young boy ran past, the Greeks on his
heels, and as he drew level with the secret courtyard

fell with a spear in his back. Priam gave a great cry then and, breaking from Hecabe's grasp, staggered out and went for the Greeks with his sword. They laughed at him and knocked his sword from his hands. Then their leader struck him down, and while some of them clustered around to give him a blow, others ran into the courtyard and dragged Hecabe away with them. She had lost all the use of her legs and looked already dead.

Asterius turned away from this sight and saw Aeneas again. Now he was not wearing any armor, but was carrying a white-bearded old man on his back, stumbling among the crowds and trying to get to safety. The Libyan said grimly, "That is his father, Anchises. But he will be lucky if he gets very far with the old man. These hounds will drag them down."

Tears started in the eyes of Asterius, and then something very strange happened. Agamemnon appeared in his gold chariot again, standing high above the crowds and shouting loudly. His voice came up clearly to the tower. He said, "Stand back, my Greeks. Let one good thing be said about us in the future. Make way for Aeneas. Let him go through the Dardanian Gate to safety. It is not often that one sees a son so loving toward his father. I grant his freedom. Who touches him, dies."

The Greeks stood back. Some of them cheered and waved their spears in honor of Aeneas, but he did not glance aside at them as he stumbled on.

The Libyan said softly, "The Lion of Mycenae has one drop of mercy left in him, then. It surprises me."

A slave woman standing by him said, "His brother Menelaus is softhearted, too. They say that he has forgiven Helen for deserting him and is hanging up leopard skins over the doors of all the noble families as a sign they are not to be touched by fire or sword."

The Libyan laughed bitterly. "Will he hang the skins over the doors of common soldiers and slaves, though? I do not think so."

Now all Troy was ablaze, sending up black smoke as from a tall chimney. The night wind caught it and swept it out to the sea. Birds flew above the smoke, crying out in terror. And from the streets below there were cries of terror, too. Men, women, and small children echoed the birds, until their cries were cut short. And at last, as dawn started slowly in the east, Troy was silent again, its buildings charred, its thatched roofs only heaps of white ash. Asterius could hear the Greeks laughing and boasting beyond the wall now, waiting with their spears to see if any survivors should crawl out of the ruined city.

Asterius was shivering and hungry; he could hardly see for the smoke in his eyes. As the morning winds grew stronger, he felt that if he did not move he would topple down from the tower into the corpse-strewn street below. So, weakly, he edged his way to the stairs and slowly went down, leaning against the wall and having to sit on the steps many times.

At last he passed through the Bull Court and saw that the great bronze beast had been thrown from its pedestal and broken. Its horned head lay at the other side of the pavement. And beside it lay Cassandra and Queen Hecabe, trussed up with chains as though they were prisoners. He tried to speak to them, but they closed their eyes and did not answer.

He did not know how to undo the chains with his frozen fingers, so he staggered past them toward the dark corridor that led to the outer steps of the palace. The wall hangings hung smoldering and ruined; even the pavements were cracked and littered with broken swords and shattered vases and shreds of clothing.

Then as he came to the door of Helen's bower he heard her voice saying, "We must find Asterius, husband. Send out soldiers to search the city for him. He may not be dead after all."

He stood in the doorway then and said, "No, I am not dead, lady. But I do not feel alive, either."

Helen rose from a stool and came to meet him, putting her arms about him as she used to. Behind her stood a tall Greek in battered armor, his helmet-crest shorn away, his black cloak hanging ragged behind him. His long sword was hacked the length of its blade, and his face and beard were caked with soot. Across his forehead was a broad open gash with the blood dried on it. He looked much like Agamemnon, but smaller and less noble.

Helen said, "This is my husband, Menelaus, the King of Sparta, boy. He has forgiven me for coming to Troy and he will be kind to you too, if you will kneel before him now."

Asterius shook his head. "I am not brave or noble, my lady," he said. "He will not hang the leopard skin outside my door."

Menelaus frowned a little and glared at him, then smiled slowly and said, "You are brave enough, boy. Few Trojans would dare speak such words to me at this moment of victory. Kneel, as Helen says, and I will spare you. You shall sail back with us to Sparta and be the slave of my daughter Hermione. She is about your age. She would like a Trojan slave as a gift from the war."

Helen smiled at him and nodded. "Kneel, Asterius," she whispered. "I would like you to come with us."

Asterius clenched his jaw and said, "Outside, in the Bull Court, the Queen Hecabe and the Princess Cassandra lie bound. I will kneel before the King of Sparta if these ladies are given their freedom."

The eyes of Menelaus grew very wide and fierce then. In his fire-blackened face they looked terrible. He began to growl, but Helen put her hand over his mouth to silence him. Then she said, "Asterius, do not sign your own death warrant, boy. Do not meddle with things that only concern great kings. Cassandra belongs to Agamemnon, the High King, and Hecabe to Odysseus. They are prisoners of war,

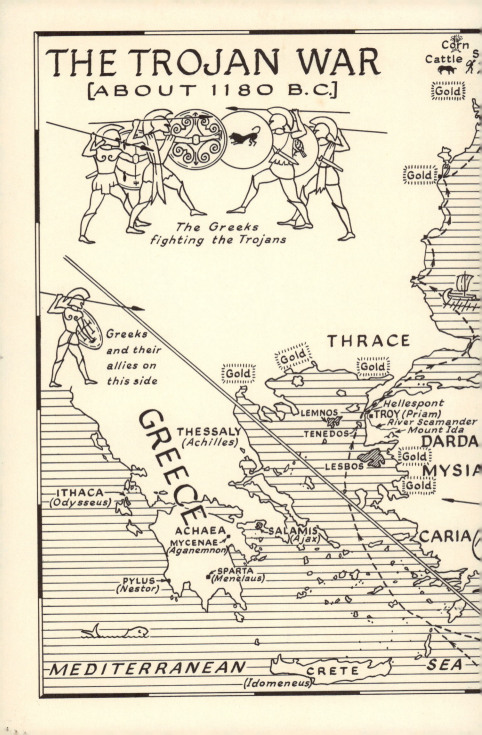

THE TROJAN WAR
[ABOUT 1180 B.C.]

The Greeks
fighting the Trojans

Corn
Cattle
S

Gold

Gold

Greeks
and their
allies on
this side

THRACE

Gold

Gold

Gold

Hellespont

TROY (Priam)

River Scamander

Mount Ida

LEMNOS

GREECE

THESSALY
(Achilles)

TENEDOS

DARDA

Gold

MYSIA

LESBOS

Gold

ITHACA
(Odysseus)

CARIA

ACHAEA

SALAMIS
(Ajax)

MYCENAE
(Aganemnon)

PYLUS→
(Nestor)

SPARTA
(Menelaus)

MEDITERRANEAN

CRETE
(Idomeneus)

SEA

important hostages. No man, not even Menelaus, could set them free."

Asterius said, "Then not even Menelaus can make me kneel, lady. I will not kneel just to become the slave of a young girl in Sparta and be thrashed and ill-treated as she pleases. I would rather die, as Hector and Paris have done. There is no more to be said."

Although he spoke so bravely, his heart was thudding and his legs almost gave way under him. He bowed his head and closed his eyes, expecting to hear the roar of Menelaus, then the swishing of his hacked bronze sword as it came down.

But all he heard was a rushing sound and the striding of feet. He felt a waft of air as though a cloak had swept past his face. Then he felt Helen touching him on the shoulder and lifting up his chin. He opened his eyes and saw that they were alone in the bower and that she was looking down and smiling sadly as she shook her head at him.

"O Asterius," she said, "you will never know how close you have stood to death this day. Do not tempt the Furies any further, my love. There is a limit to all things. You have gained your freedom by your boldness; do not ruin everything now. Do not spoil it for both of us."

She began to stroke his hair and he was so astounded by her words that he did not pull away. He said dully, "Am I free then, my lady? Am I really free?"

She nodded and smiled again. "You are as free as the air, Asterius. Menelaus swept his cloak over you as he went, to indicate that your slavery has now been wiped away. He is a noble man, though many speak harsh words of him."

He had often dreamed of being free, as though it would be a time of leaping and laughing, of great joy. But now it had come, he could not believe it. He did not even feel glad. He could only think of poor Hecabe and Cassandra, lying trussed-up in the Bull Court.

Helen drew him to her and said, "Now that you are free, will you sail to Sparta with me? Will you be my adopted son?"

But he shook his head once more and said, "I do not wish to see another Greek as long as I live, lady. If Greece is full of such folk as I saw slaying last night, then I should not be happy there."

Helen sat on the stool now and began to twist a lock of her long golden hair between her white fingers. And after a while she said, "Troy will be a deserted city for generations now. You would starve here. Where will you go? The countryside to the north and south is laid waste and is full of lawless men. They would rob and kill you."

He stood up straight then and looked her in the eye as a free man should and answered, "I will make my way toward the east to where the Hittites live. They are a good folk, I think, and one could expect justice from them. That is what I will do."

Helen nodded. "I think you are right, Asterius," she said. "But they live far from Troy and you might die before you crossed the mountains to their kingdom. Now that I am sailing home I have no further use for the horse Hippomedon. He loves you and would carry you to the Hittites safely. They are a race of horsemen and would admire such a horse and such a rider. Go to the stables now and take Hippomedon. He is yours. I shall not come with you because if I set eyes on him again, I should not be able to part with him, or with you. Go now."

Then, for the first time, he really knew that he was free. He ran to Helen and fell on his knees before her, but she drew her robe over her face and would not look at him, and when he put his hand on her arm she shrugged it away. He thought she was weeping and he did not know what to say to that.

So he turned and went from the bower, along the

dark and echoing corridors, and so out into the yard, past the scattered heap of bronze that used to belong to old Talos, and on to the stable where Hippomedon seemed to be expecting him, thumping on the ground with his great impatient hooves.